A nail, a stick and a lid

Geraldine Kaye

Illustrated by Linda Birch

BROCKHAMPTON PRESS
KNIGHT BOOKS

ISBN 0 340 19645 9 (Cased)
ISBN 0 340 19642 4 (Paper)

First published 1975 by Knight books and
Brockhampton Press Ltd, Salisbury Road, Leicester
Printed in Great Britain by Cox & Wyman Ltd,
London, Fakenham and Reading

It was Saturday and Billy's Mum
was going shopping. She said,
"I'm going to get a new shopping bag
as it's Saturday."

"Can I have the old shopping bag
as it's Saturday?" Billy said.
"It's got a hole," said June.
"Silly Billy."

Billy thought a bit.
Then he got a pin and fixed the hole.
Billy was good at fixing things.
Billy went out.

"Got your pocket money?"
John said.
"Yes," said Billy.
"Getting sweets?"
said Mike.
"No," said Billy. "I'm
getting something
for my bag."

Billy went down the
High Street.
He went to the tool shop.
There were silver hammers
in the window.

Billy went in.
"I've got five pence as it's Saturday,"
Billy said. "What can I buy?"
"You can buy a few nails," the man said.

The man shook the nails out.
They looked like little silver fish.
"Tiddlers," said Billy.

Billy put the nails in his bag.
He walked on down the High Street.
He saw lolly sticks and round tin lids
like silver moons.
Billy picked up the round tin lids and
put them in his bag.

Billy came to the park.
There were lots of children on the swings but Billy walked under the trees and picked up sticks. He put them in his bag.

"What's in your bag, Billy?" Mike said.
"Moons and things," Billy said.
"Billy's daft," said John.

Billy sat and thought a bit.
He fixed a tin lid to a stick.
He fixed it with a nail.
Billy was good at fixing things.

Billy pushed the stick along and the lid went round and round.

"What's that?" said Mike.

"It's a car," said Billy.

"We can make cars too," said Mike.
"Yes," said John. "Let's get
sticks and lids."

But all the lids and sticks
were in Billy's bag.
Billy sat on his bag.

"Give us a lid, Billy?" Mike said.
"Give us a stick, Billy?" John said.
"Lids are a penny," said Billy.

"A penny just for an old lid?"
said Mike.
"A penny for a lid and a stick
and a nail," said Billy.

"All right," said John.
"Here's a penny."
Billy gave John a lid
and a stick and a nail.
"All right then," said Mike.

Mike and John
fixed lids and sticks.
Then they ran round the park
with their cars.
"Zoom, zoom,
mine's a racing car," shouted Mike.

All the boys wanted cars.
All the boys bought lids
and sticks and nails for
a penny.
They said, "Billy's not daft."

The boys ran round and round the park.
"Zoom, zoom," they shouted.
"I've got a racing car.
Race you, Billy?"

June came to the park.
"What's in your bag, Billy?"
"Twelve pence," said Billy.
"Like a lolly as it's Saturday?"

"Green," said June.
"I like red," said Billy.
Billy bought the lollies.
Then he walked along the High Street
with his car.
"Zoom, zoom," said Billy
all the way home.

suga

If they see it we shall have to share it with them and there won't be any left for us. Mary Jane has an appetite like a horse.'

Paula grabbed the tin of toffee.

'Where shall I hide it?' she asked. 'Where will it be safe?'

'I don't care where you put it,' said Pam, 'just be quick, that's all. Put it in the bedroom if you like. Put it under the bed. Anywhere.'

Paula obeyed. And she was only just in time. As she came out of the bedroom there was a knock on the front door. The two girls tried hard to be polite to their visitors but they didn't encourage them to stay. All the time they were thinking of their precious toffee. And when at last Mary Jane's mother said she thought it was time to go, Pam and Paula didn't try to change their minds. They smiled their sweetest and escorted them to the door most graciously.

But when the door was closed they let out a shriek of delight and rushed to the bedroom.

Pam got to the bed first and looked underneath.

'Where did you leave it?' she asked.

'There!'

'But there's no toffee. You must have put it somewhere else.'

'I didn't,' said Paula, getting down on her hands and knees and looking under the bed.

'It's gone!' she cried. 'Who could have taken it?'

Just then, from far under the bed came a low growl,

followed by the sound of somebody licking a tin.

'Trixie!' cried the girls together. 'You bad dog!'

Trixie it was. And when at last they got the tin away from her it was empty. Trixie had cleaned it as thoroughly as an automatic dishwasher.

Pam and Paula looked at each other in dismay. You can guess what they were thinking about.

'Maybe we should have shared it with Mary Jane,' said Pam.

'Maybe we should,' said Paula.

How right they were!